chicken two-step

one two

one two

chicken two-step

Chicken Joy
ON REDBEAN ROAD

A BAYOU COUNTRY ROMP

by Jacqueline Briggs Martin

pictures by Melissa Sweet

Houghton Mifflin Company
Boston 2007

Every evening
a plain brown hen and a blue-headed rooster
sat on the roof of Mrs. Miser Vidrine's chicken house.
They talked about cracked corn,
the chicken two-step,
and the blue-headed roo's sonorous voice.
Some nights the rooster crowed along
with the music of Joe Beebee
that came breezing down Redbean Road.

Everybody in St. Cecilia Parish
knew of Joe Beebee.
His music set empty shoes to dancing.

In the morning the blue-headed rooster
crowed the wake-up call.
That call made the skies pinker, the corn crunchier,
and the morning glories more glorious.
The ducks and hens—even the goose—wouldn't start
work without it.
But the rooster didn't quit at sunrise.
He'd crow at grasshoppers.
He'd strut all day and crow at clouds.
The plain brown hen, who called herself Cleoma,
chased bugs, danced to that gratifying music,
and thought her world was a sweet little egg.

Then the blue-headed roo got the chicken measles.
Those were some sore-throat, flat-on-his-back days.
When the measles were done,
the roo stood up and crowed the wake-up call—
but it was no more than a hiccup.
"You'll get it back," said Miss Cleoma. "Keep trying."
The hens were all waiting. The ducks woke up to watch.
Even the egrets came close to listen.
The blue-headed roo crowed,
"Hiccup-erk."
The hens giggled. The goose laughed out loud.
The rooster buttoned his beak—and just stopped crowing.
"Try again," said Miss Cleoma.
But the roo went under a bush and stayed.
Quiet.

Mrs. Miser Vidrine, who was nothing but practical, said,
"A roo who won't wake the barnyard
is headed for stew—quiet rooster stew."
Quick, quick, Miss Cleoma and the others
clucked up a barnyard strategy.
Then she said, *"I'll* go for help.
Our roo needs music—music so good he'll remember to sing.
Where's Joe Beebee?"

When Joe Beebee was a boy
he lay in bed at night
and listened to his Uncle Willie's fiddle music
sliding past live oaks and chinaberry trees,
and into his upstairs room.
Music was quilt and pillow to that boy.

Mrs. Miser Vidrine headed out for the ax.
Two garden onions rolled into her path.
"Onions, of course," she said.
"First I'll gather onions, then the roo."

Miss Cleoma ran down Redbean Road
and didn't stop until she came to Mr. Leo Leroy
sitting on his porch, making music with spoons.
Miss Cleoma two-stepped a rooster-in-danger dance—
strutting, hiding under a bush, running in circles.
Finally she flopped flat down in the dust.
Mr. Leo Leroy understood.
"Rooster. Under a bush.
Mrs. Miser. The ax. Quiet rooster stew.
You want Joe Beebee.
He's never played for chickens.
Too busy. Joe Beebee's the best there is."

Young Joe Beebee made himself a fiddle with a
cigar box, wood, and wire from an old screen door.
"Joe Beebee, you need a real fiddle," Uncle Willie said.
"If you'll pick my corn next month, I'll buy you one."

The plain brown hen stiffened her feathers
and trotted on down Redbean Road.

pourquoi?!

Pim, pam, pum, Mrs. Miser stirred onions into the soup,
then went for the ax.
But she stumbled over a potato.
"Potatoes, of course," she said.
"Onions, potatoes, then the roo."

Soon Miss Cleoma met Mr. Cecil Wilson,
with an accordion in a sack on his back.
The plain brown hen did the rooster-in-danger two-step.
Cecil Wilson understood. "Mrs. Miser. The ax.
Quiet rooster stew," he said. "You want Joe Beebee.
He's never played for chickens. Too busy.
Joe Beebee's the best there is."

Joe Beebee played his new fiddle night and day
until he could make it sing the songs
he heard in his head.

The little brown hen aimed her beak straight ahead
and just ran faster down Redbean Road.

Pim, pam, pum, Mrs. Miser stirred
the onion and potato broth.
"Time for the ax," she said.
But she tripped on a mound of peppers.
"I am glad I thought of peppers.
Onion, potatoes, peppers, then the roo."

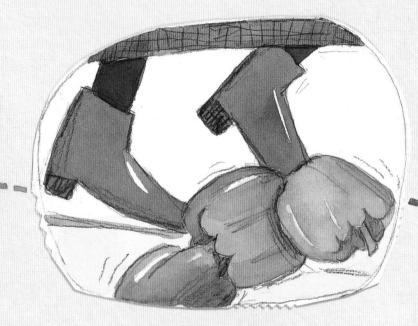

Miss Cleoma came to a place
where a red spoonbill sat in a tree
and two Brahmin cows lazed in a pasture,
and Mr. Joe Beebee himself was in the front yard,
mending his shoe and singing of sore feet.
The brown hen took a deep breath,
two-stepped the rooster-in-danger dance,
and flopped down flat.
Joe Beebee turned and went into his house.
So it's true, thought Miss Cleoma.
He won't play for chickens.

She dragged herself toward home,
lower than a lizard's chin.
Then she stopped—just sat on Redbean Road
—too sad to move.
But she hopped up when she heard Joe Beebee say,
"I'll play day or night for a good two-stepper."
Then he shook his head. "It's uphill work
bringing back a roo gone quiet, but we'll try."

The two walked along Redbean Road until
they met neighbor Pascal with a hoe in his hand.
Joe Beebee said, "Come to Mrs. Miser's.
She's having a *bal de maison*. Tell your cousins."
Cecil Wilson came along, too, and Leo Leroy with his spoons.
They saw Miss Lula hanging out clothes.
"House party at Mrs. Miser's. Bring your family."

Pim, pam, pum, at the end of Redbean Road
the chicken yard was silent, except for the bubbling stewpot.
"Onions, potatoes, peppers, beans,
okra, garlic, tomatoes . . . *now* the roo," said Mrs. Miser,
grabbing the ax.

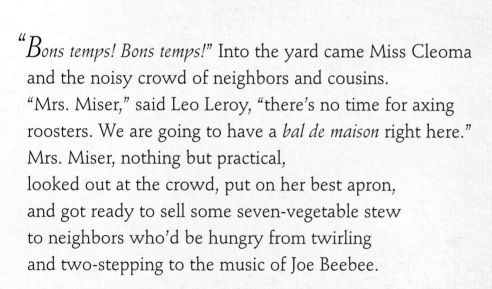

"*Bons temps! Bons temps!*" Into the yard came Miss Cleoma
and the noisy crowd of neighbors and cousins.
"Mrs. Miser," said Leo Leroy, "there's no time for axing
roosters. We are going to have a *bal de maison* right here."
Mrs. Miser, nothing but practical,
looked out at the crowd, put on her best apron,
and got ready to sell some seven-vegetable stew
to neighbors who'd be hungry from twirling
and two-stepping to the music of Joe Beebee.

When people danced to Joe Beebee's music
they forgot bad knees, tight shoes,
backaches, blisters, and beetles
that ate their sweet potatoes.
They forgot sickness, sadness, and sin.

Joe Beebee played the song about going to Texas.
His fiddle took them up
like a swing on a big old tree—with room for all:
two-legs, four-legs, wings, and fins—
up so high their worries looked small enough to stomp on.

The blue-headed roo peeked out from under the bush.
But he didn't make a sound.

Joe Beebee and the band played more songs,
songs about fat yams, lost love, good friends.
When they played that old favorite—
about waltzing on the moon—
the rooster raised his head . . .

. . . and crowed,

Qwerk-beaucoup-a-doodle-doo!

as if the world were brand new and he was off to see it.

Miss Cleoma danced on the chicken house roof
—from pure chicken joy.

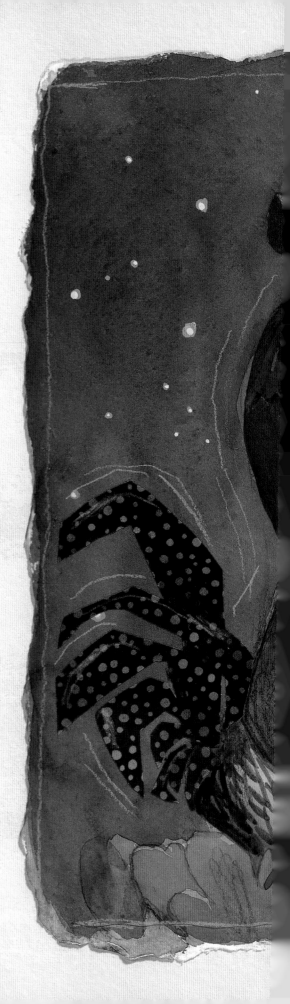

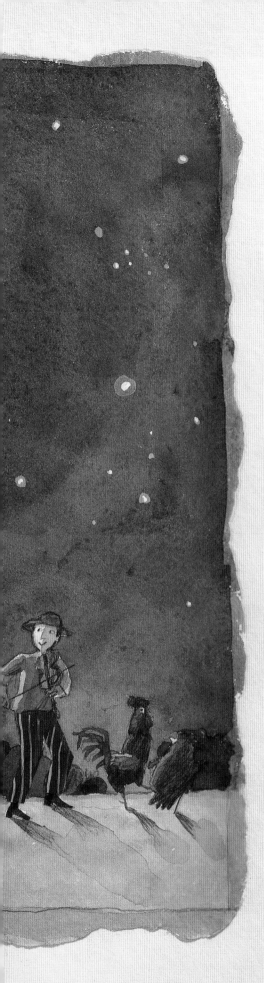

"No quiet rooster here!" said Joe Beebee.
And the vegetable stew tasted just fine.
Those dancing folks
ate it down to the bottom of the pot
—ten cents a bowl.
Then they all went home.

Nobody noticed that there were no chickens
in the chicken yard,
no ducks, no goose under the porch.
Perhaps they went to Texas.
Perhaps they went to the moon.
Mrs. Miser planted the empty yard to more vegetables.

Neighbors say they hear quacks and clucks
in the woods behind Joe Beebee's house.
Some think they see a plain brown hen and a blue-headed roo
sitting on Joe Beebee's roof,
watching the sun set through the oak woods.
They say the blue-headed roo sings along
with the music of Joe Beebee,
and that makes the skies pinker, the corn crunchier,
and the moon more glorious.

Laissez les bons temps rouler!

Author's Note

On the plains of Louisiana, Lafayette and west, there have been, and still are, musicians who play music, music so good it could make quiet roosters sing—Amédé Ardoin, Adam Fontenot, Dennis McGee, Canray Fontenot, Nathan Abshire, Alphonse "Bois-Sec" Ardoin, Iry Lejeune, the Balfa Brothers, Clifton Chenier, Boozoo Chavez, Marc Savoy, Michael Doucette, Buckwheat Zydeco, John Delafose, Christine Balfa, and many others. Recordings of this music are available on cassette tapes or compact discs. If you want to read more about this wonderful music and the people who make it, these books are a good beginning:

Cajun and Creole Music Makers. Text by Barry Jean Ancelet,
photographs by Elemore Morgan, Jr. University Press of Mississippi, 1999.

Cookin' with Queen Ida. Queen Ida Guillory and Naomi Wise. Prima Publishing, 1996.

The Kingdom of Zydeco. Michael Tisserand. Avon Books, 1998.

To Louisiana and
Gulf Coast musicians, and
to all those—two legs, four
legs, wings, and fins—
who love their music.

—J.B.M. and M.S.

www.houghtonmifflinbooks.com

The text of this book is set in Stempel Schneidler.
The illustrations are mixed media using Twinrocker handmade papers, collage, and found objects.

Library of Congress Cataloging-in-Publication Data

Martin, Jacqueline Briggs.
Chicken joy on Redbean Road / by Jacqueline Briggs Martin.
p. cm.
Summary: When a case of chicken measles steals the voice of the blue-headed rooster
who used to crow all day long, his friend, a plain brown hen, brings musicians to remind him
to sing and save him from becoming "quiet rooster stew."
ISBN 0-618-50759-0
[1. Roosters—Fiction. 2. Singing—Fiction. 3. Chickens—Fiction. 4. Parties—Fiction.
5. Farm life—Louisiana—Fiction. 6. Louisiana—Fiction.] I. Title.
PZ7.M363168Ch 2006
[Fic]—dc22
2004018779

ISBN-13: 978-0618-50759-7

Manufactured in China
SCP 10 9 8 7 6 5 4 3 2 1